W9-AVK-468

Ever After High™

The Secret Diary of

Raven Queen

Ever After High™

The Secret Diary of

Raven Queen

by Heather Alexander

LITTLE, BROWN AND COMPANY

New York Boston

This book is a work of fiction. Names, characters, places, and incidents are the product of the author's imagination or are used fictitiously. Any resemblance to actual events, locales, or persons, living or dead, is coincidental.

© 2017 Mattel, Inc. All Rights Reserved. EVER AFTER HIGH and associated trademarks are owned by and used under license from Mattel, Inc.

Cover design by Véronique Lefèvre Sweet

Hachette Book Group supports the right to free expression and the value of copyright. The purpose of copyright is to encourage writers and artists to produce the creative works that enrich our culture.

The scanning, uploading, and distribution of this book without permission is a theft of the author's intellectual property. If you would like permission to use material from the book (other than for review purposes), please contact permissions@hbgusa.com. Thank you for your support of the author's rights.

Little, Brown and Company
Hachette Book Group
1290 Avenue of the Americas, New York, NY 10104
Visit us at lb-kids.com
everafterhigh.com

First Edition: January 2017

Little, Brown and Company is a division of Hachette Book Group, Inc. The Little, Brown name and logo are trademarks of Hachette Book Group, Inc.

The publisher is not responsible for websites (or their content) that are not owned by the publisher.

Library of Congress Control Number 2016955133

ISBNs: 978-0-316-50195-8 (hardcover); 978-0-316-50194-1 (ebook)

Printed in the United States of America

LSC-H

10 9 8 7 6 5 4 3 2 1

For Kate and Keira,
the SF princesses

Diary Entry

I don't know how this diary-writing thing is supposed to work. I've never kept a diary before. I royally hope I'm doing it right. Apple White seems to love writing in hers. Every night, Apple sits cross-legged on her bed in our room at Ever After High and scribbles happy thoughts in her diary. (Wait a spell. Apple would <u>never</u> scribble. She has beautiful handwriting. Me, not so much,

but I'm working on that. Is this legible?)
I always wonder what she's writing, but
whenever I ask, she just gives me a smile
and says, "Diaries are secret, Raven!" I
know she's right, but I can't help but feel
just a little bit curious! Apple says writing
her thoughts down lets her make sense of
her story. But every time I try to rewrite my
story, everything goes _so_ wrong. And that's
why I'm trying this diary thing—maybe
it will help me make sense of my story,
what-ever-after that may be.

   This is how it all started, Diary....

   Yesterday, Baba Yaga assigned our
Magicology class homework to do over
Spring Break. Our assignment is to write
down all the spells we do, and when we get
back to Ever After High, we'll look at the

results and learn how to make the spells better or stronger. Baba Yaga floated down the aisles of our classroom on her magic pillow, passing out diaries to the rest of the class, but when she got to me, she dropped <u>two</u> journals on my desk. Everyone else got <u>one</u> journal.

Assuming she'd made a mistake, I told Baba Yaga that she had given me two journals. I tried to give one back, but she just stared at me. "You're going home today, aren't you, Miss Queen? As the daughter of the Evil Queen, I hope that you will do <u>so many</u> evil spells this Spring Break that you will easily fill two journals."

Two journals? <u>Hex no!</u> I won't fill even one journal. I will <u>not</u> be doing that many spells over Spring Break, and definitely no

evil spells! I'd like to cast no spells at all,
but I'll have to do some so I don't fail my
assignment. What I really want to do over
the break is have a fairy relaxing time.
But I couldn't say that to Baba Yaga. She
definitely wouldn't want to hear about
those plans.

My BFFAs and I have been looking
forward to this break forever after. I'm so
used to talking to my best friends every
day here at Ever After High that it will be
a little weird to not have someone to share
all my thoughts and ideas with. That's
when I got a fableous idea. I'd turn the
second journal into a diary! I can "talk" to
you, Diary, and share all my thoughts and
experiences. You'll understand what it's like
to be the daughter of the Evil Queen—to

be the girl who refuses to be evil and wants to write her own ever after.

At least, I hope you'll get it.

Spring Break starts after lunch today. Some of my friends are going home together. Briar Beauty is going home with Apple White. Rosabella Beauty is going home with Darling Charming. Cerise Hood invited me and Madeline Hatter to her house in the Dark Forest. That was an invitation I was fairy hexcited about. I feel lucky every day that I have such great BFFAs. When I was a little kid, I didn't really have that many friends, and I didn't have many sleepovers. Okay, I had zero. A lot of families don't want the daughter of the Evil Queen sleeping over at their houses. It's hard sometimes, but not everyone believes that I'm not like my mom. I understand it—I mean, my mom is a <u>legend</u> in Ever After and she's done some seriously wicked things, and I'm supposed to be just like her. But I'm not, and maybe one day all of Ever After will realize that. So the fact that Cerise's family wanted me to visit feels good. Her family isn't like other families. Everyone knows her mom is Red Riding Hood, but no one would ever guess that her dad is...Mr. <u>Badwolf</u>. (Shhh, Diary, that's a big secret! I can tell you because that's just like telling myself... but I would never-ever-after tell anyone else that.) Cerise's parents totally flipped the script!

Maddie said yes to the invitation right away. (Actually, what she said was "Do

bees kneel at tea parties? Abso-TEA-lutely!"
But that means "I'm in!" in Riddlish.) I
definitely wanted to say yes, too. It would
be hexcellent to stay up all night talking
with Maddie and Cerise. Plus, Cerise's mom
bakes the most delicious pies and cakes,
and Cerise said we'd go on a picnic in the
woods...but then I thought of home. I miss
Cook and her twins, Butternut and Pie.
I haven't seen my father, the Good King,
in forever after. I want to tell him about
all the fableous things I've been up to at
school. This was a tough choice.

Go home or visit Cerise and her family?

Then I got a hext message. My dad
invited me to sit next to him in the royal
box for the Gallant Princes on White
Horses race. The race is a big deal. All the

king's horses and all the king's men go. Princesses and fairies get dressed up and wear the most enchanting hats. Dad rides his horse around the track before the race starts. He invited me to ride next to him. He's never asked me to do that before, but he says I'm old enough now, and that he wants his spelltacular daughter by his side for all the kingdom to see.

That does it! Decision made. I'm going home for Spring Break for some overdue dad-daughter time.

Spell you later,

Raven

Chapter 1

Faybelle Thorn stood in front of the heavy door leading to the tower attic and peered down the empty hallway again. Was she alone? She had to be triple sure. It was against the rules for students to go up in the attic. If she were caught, Headmaster Grimm would probably give her detention again, and she'd spent enough time there already this year.

I won't get caught, she decided.

Faybelle hesitated for a moment. After the last time she'd sneaked up there, she'd pinkie-promised herself that she'd never-ever-after go again. But Dark Fairies are known to break promises. Even promises they make to themselves.

Faybelle recited a fairy spell, and the heavy chains crisscrossing the door immediately turned as bendy as gummy dragons. She pushed them aside and opened the door.

Faybelle's skin prickled as she ran up the narrow spiral staircase. Enchanting the door and being inside the dusty tower attic wouldn't get her into *that* much trouble. But what she was doing in the attic would—talking to *Her*. Even her mom, the Dark Fairy who'd cursed Sleeping Beauty to slumber for one hundred years, wouldn't approve. Faybelle didn't want her mom to be angry, but she couldn't help herself. Visiting with the Evil Queen made her feel brave and special. She was the

Villain Club president and already Ever After High's Fairy-to-Fear, but if the students knew that she was talking to *Her*, they'd be royally petrified.

Just thinking about all that fear made the tips of her wings tingle.

But no one could know. Ever.

Faybelle was wicked, but she wasn't stupid. The Evil Queen was locked up in mirror prison and hidden away in the attic for fairy good reason. She'd rampaged Wonderland, and then that one time she destroyed Ever After High when Dragonsport was brought back to the school...with Faybelle's help. But Faybelle really learned her lesson that time. The Evil Queen's out-of-control evil was dangerously off-book. Even Faybelle knew she needed to stay inside the mirror from now on. But it couldn't hurt to just talk to her....

The Evil Queen had so much knowledge about dark magic, much more than even Faybelle's teachers. If she was going to grow up to be the most evil villain of all time, she needed to learn from the current master. Stories would be written about Faybelle Thorn. Movies would be made, her name illuminated in fairy lights.

Faybelle tucked a strand of hair behind her ear, straightened her shoulders, and shook out her wings. One quick visit, then she'd head home for Spring Break. A lot of girls were pairing off for sleepovers. As usual, no one had invited her. No one in her family ever got invitations, which was odd considering that her mother had cursed Sleeping Beauty because she was left off a party list. You'd think they'd learn! But no worries. It was all part of her story.

Faybelle entered the silent attic. Cobwebs hung from the shadowy ceiling. Dust floating up from piles of forgotten items tickled her nose. Her heart thumped wildly, but she kept going. She was the daughter of the Dark Fairy. Nothing could stop her. She marched up to the magic mirror in the center of the room.

At first, all she saw was her reflection in the shimmering glass: glossy blond hair held back in a thorny ponytail; her cheerhexing captain's uniform with her iridescent fairy wings poking out from her back.

"Um . . . Hi . . . Hello there?"

Faybelle was never quite sure how to start. Did Raven Queen have a special way to summon her mother when she had her school-approved visits? Some kind of magic-mirror-on-the-wall rhyme? Faybelle would never ask, not that Raven would be cool enough to just tell her. Actually, Raven would probably tell Headmaster Grimm. What a waste of a destiny. Also, she and Raven weren't exactly the closest of friends. It was a shame, really. Together, the daughters of the two most notorious villains could've wreaked hexcellent havoc. Faybelle wished Raven would get on the right page already.

Faybelle crossed her arms and peered into the mirror. "Anyone there?"

"Of course I'm here. Where do you think I'd be?" With a puff of purple, the Evil Queen materialized in the mirror. She wore high-heel satin slippers and a royal-purple silk robe that was belted around her waist. Tendrils of her jet-black hair escaped from a plush towel wrapped around her head. She peeled slices of cucumber off her eyes. "I was having a spa day. I don't plan to wither and grow wrinkled here."

"You look great—truly fableous," Faybelle said eagerly.

"Of course I look great. I'm gorgeous!" The Evil Queen peered around Faybelle. "You're alone again?"

Faybelle nodded. She knew the Evil Queen was looking for her daughter. She had the feeling that Raven didn't visit much.

The Evil Queen sighed, then narrowed her eyes at Faybelle. "I guess you'll do. I can't be picky about my visitors."

"Uh, thanks." The Evil Queen made her strangely tongue-tied.

"What did you bring me?" The Evil Queen eyed Faybelle's empty hands. "Nothing? Didn't your mother teach you manners? No more books?"

Faybelle had recently made a habit of borrowing books from the Vault of Lost Tales and giving them to the Evil Queen. "Er, sorry. With Spring Break coming up, the library was too busy for me to sneak into the Vault again without getting caught. Those step-librarians really do have eyes on the back of their heads!"

"You're…sorry?" The Evil Queen turned up her nose. "Has anyone even considered that I may desire a vacation, too? A change of scenery, perhaps?"

Faybelle bounced on the toes of her silver sneakers. "I heard Raven's going back home."

"A week with the Good King. How boring! My daughter needs to cause some havoc. Raise the roof. Shake the trees. Walk on the wild side. You know what I mean?"

"I do, but Raven's into being *good*." Faybelle sneered.

"Oh please!" the Evil Queen said, rolling her violet eyes. "Raven is just experimenting. She will come to embrace her destiny."

"It might take a long time." Faybelle had seen Raven's determined expression when she refused to sign the book on Legacy Day. That girl was annoyingly serious about her choice.

"I can wait." The Evil Queen paced back and forth, back and forth. Then she threw up her hands. "No, I can't! Raven has played her silly game long enough. My daughter *must* embrace her evil destiny! There's no time to waste. You must help me help Raven discover her true self."

"Of course." Faybelle didn't particularly want to help Raven, but she was eager to prove herself to the Evil Queen.

The Evil Queen's eyes flashed with hex-citement as she pulled a familiar slim red book from a pocket in her robe. Faybelle had taken it from Giles Grimm's underground library. Students weren't allowed to check out those books, but Faybelle wasn't big on rules, so she'd swiped it for the Evil Queen. Besides, where was the harm? It was such a small book. No one would miss it.

"I have just the spell." The Evil Queen opened the book and pointed with her long, lacquered fingernail. "This curse ignites the evil inside one who is truly wicked in her core. This will be the spark my Raven needs."

Faybelle squinted at the curse written in fancy calligraphy. Her eyes traveled to the warning in capital letters at the bottom of the page.

CERTIFIED FOR USE ON TROLLS ONLY!*
*Results May Vary.

"Um, I don't think that spell is meant to be used on people. Raven isn't a troll—at least not in any way I can prove. What if it doesn't work?"

The Evil Queen gave a haughty laugh. "I possess the strongest magic in all of Ever After! If I want a spell to work, it will work! Raven's evilness is as deep and powerful as my own. It just needs a little...push."

Would this curse finally draw Raven to the evil side? Faybelle wasn't sure, but a Dark Fairy never turned down an opportunity to do evil. She leaned into the mirror. "What do you need me to do?"

+ ✦ ✦

Ten minutes later, Faybelle flew into the crowded Castleteria. Outside, gilded carriages lined the long driveway, waiting to whisk students to all the corners of the kingdom for Spring Break. Students hurried to finish lunch before saying good-bye. It took only a second for Faybelle to spot Raven's long purple-and-black hair. She was sitting at her usual table with Madeline Hatter and Cedar Wood. Faybelle flew toward them purposefully.

"Hi, Faybelle! We saved you a seat."

"When are you leaving? I'm going to miss you *soooo* much."

"I got you a hextra cup of blackberry pudding!"

Faybelle waved at the six loyal cheerhexing fairies on her squad without much care. Even though they'd saved her usual seat at the head of the table, she swept past them toward Raven. Raven's princess pea-butter sandwich lay untouched on her tray as she finished telling a story.

"...and that's what happened the first time I rode a dragon."

Faybelle glanced at the hickory-dickory-dock-clock on the wall. Soon it would strike one and the mouse would run out, signaling the end of lunch. For the Evil Queen's plan to work, Faybelle couldn't let Raven return to her room right away.

The loudspeaker crackled and the voice of Headmaster Grimm boomed: "Students, I want to wish you a safe and happily-ever-after Spring Break. All rooms must be clean before you leave. Momma Bear will be coming by for room inspections. Students in Mr. Badwolf's General Villainy class are instructed to hand in their thronework immediately, as Mr. Badwolf will be departing earlier than planned."

Raven reached into her book bag, and Faybelle knew just what to do. She cheered under her breath:

What do you say, what do you know?

Look high, look low.

Where did Raven's thronework go?

With wicked satisfaction, Faybelle stepped back.

"Wait a spell!" Raven's brow furrowed as she flipped through the papers and books in her bag. "Where's my thronework? It was here a second ago."

"Are you sure you put it in your bag?" asked Cedar, the daughter of Pinocchio.

"I'm sure." Raven bit her lip and looked again, more slowly this time. "At least, I was sure."

"I know how you feel." Maddie nodded. "I lost my hat."

"The one with the teapot?" Cedar widened her eyes. "It's on your head."

"Wonderlandiful!" Maddie clapped her hands with delight. "If you can't see something, it's hard to be sure it's there. Sometimes I wonder about my ears and my eyebrows."

"Your ears and eyebrows are right where they should be." Cedar grinned. Maddie was the daughter of the Mad Hatter, which sometimes led to her making some outrageous observations.

"Good to know!" Maddie beamed. Then she gave her ears a good tug, just in case.

"I can see everything in my bag." Raven sat back, puzzled. "Where could my thronework be?"

"Backward go to need you," said Maddie.

"Is that Riddlish?" Raven asked. Maddie often spoke in the native language of Wonderland, where she'd grown up. Most people thought it sounded like nonsense, but Maddie insisted it made perfect sense.

"No, silly goose! I was just speaking backward, because you need to *go* backward," she said with a wink.

"Huh? Walk backward?"

Maddie let out a big laugh. "Oh, I adore walking backward! You can always see where you came from. But you need to reverse the order of your day."

"Where did you go before you came here, Raven?" Cedar translated.

Raven remembered putting her thronework in her bag when she left her room this morning. After that, she'd brought her dragon, Nevermore, to the dragon stable beyond the sword-training meadow. Nevermore would spend the vacation there with the other dragons. Then she'd gone down to the cauldron room to return a mixing spoon. Had she left her thronework there?

"Be right"—Raven paused to take a few big bites of her sandwich—"back!" She raced for the door.

"Don't worry!" Cedar called after her. "It will all work out in The End."

Raven hoped so. She'd never failed to turn in her thronework. Even when Nevermore had once eaten it, she'd stayed up late and done the Home Evilnomics assignment again. Would she get a bad grade if she couldn't find it before her teacher left?

Faybelle snickered as Raven ran down to the basement. Perfect! Raven Queen would be busy for a while—long enough for Faybelle to put the Evil Queen's curse into place. She sneaked out the Castleteria door and was about to make her way to the section of the school that housed the girls' dorm rooms . . . but then she remembered a crucial piece of her plan. She used her magic to retrieve a small white bakery box she'd hidden earlier in a supply closet. Faybelle opened her wings and flew toward Apple and Raven's room, landing gently in front of the door a few moments later. Faybelle reached to twist the doorknob, when she heard singing.

"Z, y, x, w, v, u, t, s, r, q . . ."

A girl at the opposite end of the hall was walking backward and singing the alphabet backward. Faybelle narrowed her gaze. Madeline Hatter, of course. Who else would be doing everything all topsy-turvy? She must've left the Castleteria early, too.

Faybelle slipped her hand off the doorknob, just as Maddie passed.

"Olleh, Ellebyaf!" Maddie called out.

Faybelle had no idea what Maddie was babbling about, nor did she really care. She considered saying hello but decided against it. If she suddenly started acting nice, Maddie might get suspicious. Faybelle glared instead.

"Have a great Gnirps Kaerb! Now, where was I? Oh yes. *P, o, n, m, l...hmmm,* that doesn't quite sound as fun on my tongue as *l, m, n, o....*" Maddie's voice trailed off as she turned the corner and disappeared down a different hall.

Faybelle quickly opened the door. It was easy to tell which side of the room belonged to Raven. Raven's dark furniture had thorny spikes and purple pillows and sheets, while Apple's bed had a fluffy white canopy and red and gold accents.

"A little something, from your mom," Faybelle muttered as she placed the white box in the middle of Raven's bed. She hurried out, closing the door tightly behind her.

Would the little "present" make Raven evil? Or maybe it would turn her into a troll? It was win-win as far as Faybelle was concerned. Oh, how she'd love to see Raven Queen as a troll!

Faybelle returned to the Castleteria just as the clock struck one. Students filed out, hugging good-bye and promising to hext during their time away. She stayed to the side, secretly watching as Raven rushed over to Cedar. Her face was flushed and her hair fell into her eyes.

"Did you find it?" Cedar asked.

"No!" Raven bent over, huffing and puffing. "I looked everywhere. The cauldron room up to the Charmitorium over to the meadow and then back down to the Lost and Crowned office. What am I going to do?"

"You need to tell Mr. Badwolf the truth." Cedar pointed to the main doors. The teacher was walking out of the school. "Honesty is the best policy."

"I know." Raven wished she didn't have to start her vacation on such a sour note. "It's not fair. I'd deserve to fairy-fail if I didn't do my throncwork, but I *did* do it."

Faybelle sighed and frowned. Messing up Raven's grades was fairy tempting. But what if she was sent to Headmaster Grimm's office as punishment for not turning in her assignment? Then there might not be time for Raven to go find her "present."

Under her breath, she cheered:

S-T-O-P at the door,
L-O-S-T no more!

Give one more look,
between the books!

Raven started toward Mr. Badwolf, but she hesitated as he stopped suddenly in the open doorway to answer a question from Kitty Cheshire. Raven opened her book bag again. "I have the strangest feeling that I should take another look. I know that sounds crazy. I mean, it's not—" She gasped and, from between two hextbooks, slid out her thronework. "Wait a spell! This wasn't here before."

Cedar shrugged. "You must've missed it."

"I'm losing my crown!" Raven laughed with relief. She hurried to hand it to her teacher, and then she hugged her friends good-bye. Raven was surprised when Faybelle, who was hovering nearby, hugged her, too.

Raven's stomach grumbled as she returned to her room. She'd had only a few bites of her sandwich at lunch and wished she'd thought to grab an apple from the fruit bowl in the Castleteria.

Pushing open her door, she was greeted by a deafening silence. No songbirds chirped at the window. No Apple singing to little birds from the windowsill. Apple's hybrid carriage had picked her and Briar up at the beginning of lunch for her journey home. Raven missed her roommate already. She was whistling a tune Apple liked when she suddenly spotted a white box on her deep-purple satin comforter.

"What's this?" Raven lifted a small, glittery card from the box. "It says, 'Eat me.'"

Raven opened the lid and inhaled the sweet, sugary scent of pink thronecake. *How thoughtful of Maddie to have left this for me,* she thought. Or maybe Apple had left it as a good-bye treat. Apple knew thronecake was one of her favorite foods.

What good friends she had!

Raven couldn't wait. She gobbled down the thronecake and licked the last bit of sticky frosting from her lips. All of a sudden, tiny green lights flickered before her eyes and a buzzing filled her ears. She felt strangely light-headed and sat on her bed.

"Wow! Massive sugar rush!" Perhaps she shouldn't have eaten the treat so fast.

The woozy feeling passed after a moment, and she reached for her purple velvet duffel bag. Her own carriage waited outside. She was ready for Spring Break to begin.

Diary Entry

How are you feeling, Diary? I'm feeling kind of weird. I'm not sneezing and I don't have a sore throat, but I guess it's just that I don't feel like myself tonight. If Maddie were here, she'd ask me who I felt like, but I don't know. I just feel kind of wishy-washy and strange.

My welcome-home dinner did not go at all as I'd hexpected. Ooglot, our family ogre, waddled outside to greet me when my carriage pulled up to the castle this afternoon. He picked up my bags and then he did the weirdest thing. He inched closer to me and inhaled really deeply. It was almost like he was sniffing me... super weird! Cook hugged me tight and pinched my cheeks, and I played hide-and-seek with Butternut and Pie on the wide lawn until we got called in for dinner. I raced through the Great Hall and into the dining room to see my dad. He was sitting by himself at the end of the long table that was definitely fit for a king. I gave him a big hug and sat right next to him.

Cook served us a scrumptious meal of fried chicken, beanstalk casserole, and plum pudding. My father told me about the latest happenings of the kingdom. Everyone comes to him with their problems, because he's so kind and wise. There was a building-code problem and houses made of straw were being blown down. He ruled that brick houses should be built instead. A boy had attempted to jump over a candlestick and burned his big toe. My father had visited him in the hospital.

Then it was my turn. I had SO much to tell him about Ever After High. I had just gotten through describing my Muse-ic Class when a trumpet sounded. The dining room doors swung open, and one of the king's footmen appeared. Dad stopped eating as the footman unrolled a parchment scroll. "Hear ye, hear ye, I come with a message!" he boomed. "The cow has jumped over the moon, and a pig has flown up in the air. What say you?"

My dad considered the issue and then swiftly reached a decision. He ruled that nighttime kite-flying should be halted until the sky was cleared of all animals. The footman departed, and I went back to telling him about Maddie, Cerise, Apple, and all my other friends at school. A few minutes later, another footman appeared with another problem. Once that one had gone, another showed up. It went on like this throughout our entire dinner. My dad was so busy solving problems that he barely had time to listen to me. I got a little frustrated and, before I could stop myself, I let out a strange, almost troll-like burp.

Totally weird!

Dad and I both laughed. Where had that crazy sound come from? I'm telling you, Diary, I'm not quite myself. My dad apologized for all the interruptions, and I do understand—the kingdom needs him, and I love that he never lets his people down. That's what makes him such a <u>good</u> king. It makes no sense that I felt so frustrated, even just for a fairy quick moment.

Dad promised we'd find some quality father-daughter time soon.

I'm going to bed now. I hope I feel more like myself tomorrow.

Spell you later, Diary.

Raven

Chapter 2

Hello, sleepyhead!" Cook greeted Raven late the next morning as she walked into the kitchen, letting out a big yawn.

"It was so hard getting out of bed this morning." Raven pulled a stool up to the kitchen counter. Even after a good night's sleep, she still felt a bit off-kilter. Maybe some breakfast would do the trick.

She spread butter onto a freshly baked blueberry muffin and took a big bite. Purple berry juice stained her lips. Cook pointed to the purple skirt that Raven wore with a black tank top and lace-up silver sandals. "Your lips match your skirt."

"Blueberries are like castlemade lip gloss," Raven said. She looked out the open window toward the towering cliffs and the sea beyond. "Where's Dad?"

"Out and about." Cook wiped her hands on her white apron. "He's a busy man, you know."

"I know." Raven's smile faded. "I was just hoping to spend some time with him today."

Cook consulted the master schedule on her MirrorPhone. "It says here that he has an important lunch meeting. After that the royal tailor is fitting him for new knickers." Her blue eyes twinkled. "Look! He set aside dinnertime with you, and he said no footmen are allowed in."

"That's perfect." Raven quickly finished the rest of her muffin. "Let's make it a party! Oh, I remember this one time you made brambleberry pie and Dad loved it. Would you mind making it for him tonight? And speaking of brambleberries, I saw this hex-cellent dish on a spellebrity chef show that used brambleberries for the sauce, and..." Her voice trailed off as she saw Cook frown. "What's wrong?"

"I have so much to do today already. I need to prepare the food for his lunch meeting and—"

"That's okay, Cook. Is there a recipe for the brambleberry pie? Maybe I can make it myself." Raven hopped off the stool, suddenly energized. "I can definitely handle this. And I promise I won't get in your way. I can pull out the ingredients." She opened the pantry. "See, here's the flour and sugar and salt." She dropped them on the counter, then bent over to open a cabinet. "Here's one mixing bowl. Here's another. Do we need more?" Raven whirled around to the spice rack. "Cinnamon. Basil. Maybe some paprika? *Hmmm*, what else? Oh, definitely eggs and butter!" She hurried toward the refrigerator as Cook chuckled in amusement.

"We need pans." Raven opened another cabinet and piled five pans in her arms. "I forgot milk." She pivoted back to the refrigerator and her foot slipped, sending the pans into the air. One by one, they clattered to the tile floor. Raven toppled, too, landing alongside the pans.

"Are you okay?" Cook hurried to help her up.

"Oh, I'm fine," Raven assured her while laughing at her own clumsiness.

Cook laughed, too. "You're like a troll let loose in my kitchen."

"I'm sorry. Not sure what got into me! I just got hexcited." Raven gathered the pans.

"I can see how much this dinner means to you." Cook pulled out a piece of paper and a quill pen. "Let's start at the beginning and create a menu. Then we can see what goes into the oven first. I need order in my kitchen if I'm going to cook your special dinner."

"Oh, thank you!" Raven hugged Cook, and together they decided on a menu of roast beef, pea soup, curds-and-whey fritters, chopped salad, and a big fairy-food cake since there were no brambleberries in the kitchen for a pie. As Cook began to chop the vegetables for the king's lunch and the dinner party, her twins scampered into the kitchen in a whirlwind of noise and energy.

"Tag, you're it!"

"No way, you're it!"

The boys raced around the room, each swinging his chubby arms wildly in an effort to reach the other. In minutes, the pans Raven had piled onto the counter crashed to the floor again.

"Oh dear. I don't think I'll ever get all this food prepared with these two underfoot." Cook sighed.

"I can babysit," Raven offered. The twins let out a cheer.

"That's a big help. I'm off to the henhouse for eggs. We need more than this carton. Maybe the three of you can shell the peas?"

"Sure, I think we can handle that!" Raven replied.

Cook smiled gratefully. "Just make sure not to take your eyes off them!" Cook whispered to Raven. "They'll make a mess faster than you can say 'Happily Ever After!'"

"Got it!" Raven said. She sat the twins at the round table and showed them how to pull the tiny peas from the pods. They got the hang of it quickly. A few moments later, Raven began having an unfamiliar feeling: impatience. Suddenly, she couldn't wait to finish with the pile of peas.

"Let's have a race," she told the twins. "The first one to finish their pile of peas wins. Ready, set, go!" Raven's mind spun as she worked. She thought of the yummy menu. *There really is a lot of food for Cook to prepare. Oh dear. Maybe this wasn't a good idea. I just made Cook's busy day so much harder. Is Cook angry at me for creating hextra work? That would be horrible. No, no!* She shook her head. *Don't be silly. Cook understands. She has to . . . right?*

"Look, Raven! You lost!" Butternut cried with glee, pointing at Raven's pile, which hadn't grown any smaller. She was so deep in thought that she'd just stopped shelling peas altogether.

Raven pushed her pea pods toward the twins. "Finish for me? I'll be right back. No one get into any trouble."

She sprinted out the back door and toward the henhouse. She would tell Cook that they would simplify the menu. She didn't want to be too demanding. A few feet away from the house, the twins' delighted squeals rang out through the open window.

Raven paused. Could they be that happy shelling peas? Doubtful. She glanced toward the henhouse and back at the kitchen. The laughter grew louder. That did it! She raced back inside.

"Oh my godmother!" Raven cried out. The mischievous twins had found the big bag of flour. They scooped and tossed fistfuls into the air. Butternut grabbed the bag and struggled to lift it up over his brother's head....

"Stop! Freeze!"

The twins froze, and for a moment everything was still, until Butternut lost his grasp on the heavy bag. They all watched a blizzard of flour blanket every surface. The kitchen looked like the Snow Queen's winter wonderland. Butternut's orange hair was dusted with white, and Pie's pudgy arms and legs resembled chicken cutlets floured and ready to fry in a pan.

Raven wanted to scold them, but it was all her fault. Her only job had been to keep the rambunctious twins out of trouble. She had messed it up, and now Cook's kitchen was a royal disaster. Guilt hardened the blueberry muffin into a brick in her stomach. What was going on with her? Why in Ever After had she left the twins alone in the kitchen?

"We need to clean up fairy fast." She handed each boy a dish towel and pushed up her sleeves. Cook prided herself on her spotless kitchen, often bragging that the floor was so clean you could eat off it. "You two do the table. I've got the counter." Raven wiped her damp towel through the thick layer of flour, creating a gloppy paste.

She swooped again in a wider arc, and her hand knocked the carton of eggs on the counter, sending them flying into the air. She let out a startled cry and tried to dive for them—but she wasn't fast enough.

Splat!

One dozen eggs exploded on the flour-dusted floor. Yellow yolks oozed from cracked shells, spreading in a sticky puddle, seeping into her sandals and tickling her toes. Raven had just made the mess a hundred times worse. What was wrong with her today?

Butternut's cries jolted her out of her daze. "*Whee!* Waterslide!"

"No! Egg-slide!" Pie joined his brother, sliding on baking pans through the yolk puddle, smearing gunk across the floor.

"Stop!" Raven raised her hand like a troll guarding a bridge.

The twins stopped sliding and pointed at her hand. Purple sparks crackled from Raven's fingertips. When she was angry, magic pulsed its way out of her.

I can do a cleanup spell, she realized suddenly.

Raven's gaze landed on the broken eggs and the near-empty flour bag. Even better—

she'd use magic to recycle the flour and eggs and bake a cake. Cook would get a spotless kitchen, wouldn't waste food, and wouldn't have to spend time baking. A win-win-win!

Clean and bake,
Create a cake.
Clean the floor,
Crumbs no more.

Magical energy exploded from her fingers, and for a moment, the kitchen clouded in a haze of purple. Raven smelled something baking. She squinted as the fog cleared. Had her spell worked?

The egg yolk mess was gone. The floor and counter were no longer covered with flour. She'd done it! She peeked into the oven. It was empty. Where was the cake?

"We're kings of the mountain!"

Raven whirled around. The twins sat atop an absolutely *enormous* pile that took up most of the kitchen. Where had *that* come from? She edged closer and pushed her fingers in it. Was it made of sand? Gravel? No, but it smelled familiar. She took a tentative taste, and her eyes widened.

Cake crumbs! She'd conjured the Mount Ever After of cake crumbs. Her spell was a fairy-fail!

What now? Could she mush the crumbs together and mold them into a cake? With a thick layer of frosting, maybe no one would ever know. Raven shook her head. That would never work. The pile of crumbs almost reached the ceiling!

"Oh!" Cook gasped as she pushed open the door.

Raven cringed. "I can explain—"

"I'd rather not know." Cook sighed as she lifted her twins off the crumbs. "You are clearly your mother's daughter in the kitchen. She always caused a whirlwind when she came in here. What if you focus on decorations and leave the baking to me?"

She shooed Raven and the twins from the kitchen. Then she called to the ogres to bring shovels and wheelbarrows to cart out the crumbs.

Diary Entry

I really need to talk. I tried to cast a
cleanup spell after creating a royal mess
in the kitchen, but my spell created an
even bigger mess. It took the ogres and
Cook over an hour to clear out the mess I
made, so she didn't have time to prepare
the Coronation Chicken Salad for Dad's
lunch meeting. He had no choice but to
make a reservation at Ye Olde Restaurant

in the village instead of eating in his own castle. He's been gone all afternoon!

I can't stop thinking about what Cook said. <u>Am I really like my mother?</u> I know I look like her, but I'm not like her on the inside...am I? Is it possible there are crumbs of wickedness in me?

I wish my friends were here so I could talk to them. What would they say? Apple would remind me that even though I caused some problems today, I could never-ever-after cause as many problems as the Evil Queen. And Maddie would tell me...actually, I have no idea what Maddie would tell me because it would probably be in Riddlish, but I'm sure she'd make me feel better. I <u>always</u> feel like myself when I'm with my friends. The one other thing that can make me feel like myself, oddly enough, is a visit to my mother. It might sound weird, but when I see her, I feel fairy, fairy certain that I'm nothing like her!

Wait! I just got an idea! I'll visit my mother. She might be able to snap me out of this strange funk. Wish me luck, Diary!

Spell you later!

Raven

Chapter 3

Raven entered her mother's old bedroom, where the mirror was kept. As far as she knew, only two mirrors could access the Evil Queen. One was kept behind a heavily chained door in the tower attic of Ever After High. The other was in the Queen's Wing in the Other Side of the Castle.

When Raven was little, she loved to watch the Evil Queen at her vanity table as she got ready for a dinner party. Sitting along-side her, Raven would gaze at her mother's reflection in the mirror as she brushed her glossy jet-black hair with a silver brush and then applied shimmering poisonous-plum lipstick. She would touch Raven's lips with the lipstick, adding a touch of matching color. Side by side, they would smile.

Now her mother was *inside* the mirror. Raven waited without saying a word. Somehow, the Evil Queen always knew when her daughter was there.

"Namaste, darling!" Her mother appeared in the mirror. Her dark hair was swept into a high ponytail and a stretchy metallic headband rested on her forehead. She wore a fairy stylish black zip-up hoodie and black stretch pants. "I just finished my yoga class. I'm feeling so zen. We must stay healthy, or our dark powers fade. How are you feeling these days?"

"I'm fine," Raven replied. She wasn't used to her mother being so cheerful. Usually, the Evil Queen complained about being locked away in mirror prison and reminded Raven over and over again about how disappointing it was that she was choosing not to follow her destiny.

"Fine? What's *fine* mean?" The Evil Queen eyed her daughter up and down. "Any evil stirrings? Rumblings of terror? Visions of darkness?"

Raven shifted uncomfortably. When she was little, her mother could tell her exact temperature by placing her cheek on her forehead, but now a thick pane of magic glass separated them. How did her mother know she wasn't feeling quite right?

"I'm *not* feeling evil," Raven insisted. "We've talked about this so many times. I'm not going down that path."

"You must be feeling even a tiny bit more wicked today than you were yesterday." The Evil Queen raised her arched eyebrows quizzically, as if not quite believing her. "No? Then maybe you're doing some little wicked things? Just...casually?"

The kitchen disaster flashed before Raven's eyes. Had that happened because she was wicked? No, that happened because she hadn't been paying attention to the twins and then her spell backfired.

This wasn't working out as she'd planned. Seeing her mother was supposed to make her feel better. She steeled herself and stood up straight, looking her mother in the eyes.

"I'm all good," Raven replied confidently, but the slight waver in her voice gave her away.

"Ah, then there *is* something amiss." Her mother's gaze bore into her like a hex-ray, searching for the evil she had ignited with her curse.

The Evil Queen was confused. No darkness simmered in her daughter's soul. What had happened to the curse? She inhaled sharply and worry creased her brow. "You haven't been sitting under bridges? Refusing people safe passage? You're not feeling... troll-ish, are you?"

"Hexcuse me?" Raven replied, laughing. "You're starting to sound as silly as Maddie."

The Evil Queen forced out a sharp laugh. "Yes, yes, just trying out some Riddlish. You know how I feel about those Wonderlandians."

"That's not funny." Raven grew serious. She hated that her own mother had invaded

Wonderland and forced her best friend and many others from their home. "What you did to Wonderland was unforgiveable and pure evil."

"Exactly!" She pointed her finger at Raven. "You, my dear, are capable of that delicious darkness, too. It's inside you. It's your destiny. You're just like me. Just look at you— you're still my mini-me."

Raven recoiled. "I may look like you on the outside, but I'm like Father on the inside."

The Evil Queen snorted. "How is your good ol' dad? Tell me. *Where* is he?" She was wise enough to know that Raven wouldn't be talking with her if her father was around to entertain her.

"He's great. He's really busy solving all the problems in the kingdom," Raven answered with pride.

"Some things never change. He never knows how to say no to his loyal subjects." She placed both hands over her heart. "Your mother is always here for you, my sweet."

"That's because you can't leave," Raven pointed out.

"You're missing the point!" she hissed. "I always put you first. When you were a baby, I always made sure you had the best nannies taking care of your every need. And if one of them dared to question me, I'd curse her with ogre breath for a week! Let me tell you, those nannies learned very quickly how to properly care for you!"

"That's horrible!" Raven's stomach turned at the thought of the poor nannies.

"No, that's a mother's love." The Evil Queen beamed proudly. "You just wait. Your evil will bloom soon. Just like mine."

"Enough!" Raven whirled away from the mirror, clenching her fists. She didn't like arguing with her mother, but she'd gotten what she'd wanted. She felt back in control.

Sort of.

The Evil Queen gave a satisfied grin as Raven stormed away. She'd seen the purple sparks that flashed from her daughter's fists. It wasn't the intense evil that she'd been hexpecting to see, but it was a start. The curse would take proper hold in due time. The Evil Queen was sure of it.

Raven hurried down to the dining room, more determined than ever to throw the best surprise dinner party for her father. He deserved a nice, relaxing meal after all his hard work. At their dinner she'd have his full attention, and they'd finally be able to catch up.

She surveyed the large dining room with fresh eyes, now that she'd been away at school. No one had used the room for a party in a fairy long time. The tapestries on the gray stone walls had begun to fade, and the purple crushed-velvet chairs had grown threadbare. The slight amber glow of the brass chandelier failed to brighten the dark corners. The room was looking fairy dreary.

Raven pulled back the shutters to let the warm sunlight filter in. She found a black lace tablecloth folded in a cupboard and smoothed it over the large table. She set out delicate china plates, etched with the black-and-silver family crest; heavy sterling knives and forks; crystal water goblets; and tall candlesticks. She cut blooming white roses from the thorniest bushes in their royal garden to create a centerpiece, and strung garlands of sweet-smelling lilacs along the walls. Then she folded two pieces of paper. On one, in purple ink, she wrote *Raven*. On the other, she wrote *Father*. She placed them side by side on the table.

She hexted the Fiddlers Three on her MirrorPhone, but they were booked to play a concert that night on the other side of the kingdom. Curses! She quickly rounded up three house ogres. They stood at attention in front of her.

"Do you think you could be my Fiddlers Three?" she asked, handing them violins she'd uncovered in a closet. She hummed the melody she wanted them to play, but she soon discovered that ogres are not at all musical. In fact, they are painfully out of tune. Their attempts at fiddling sounded like a chorus of cranky cats.

The dinner gong chimed, leaving Raven no choice. She enchanted the fiddles to play her father's favorite songs. No longer needed, the ogres scurried back to their basement rooms, but not before giving the air a curious sniff. *They must smell Cook's delicious dinner,* Raven decided.

Indeed, delicious smells wafted in from the kitchen as Raven perched on the edge of her chair, eagerly hexpecting her father's entrance. She couldn't wait to see the smile on his face.

Raven waited. The fiddles fiddled. She waited some more.

Then Cook appeared. All the happiness drained from Raven's face as Cook handed her a note printed on royal stationery.

My dearest daughter,

I am so very sorry, but I will not be home for dinner tonight. You can order in pizza, if you wish. Get as many toppings as you desire.

I have been called to help out far, far away. Jack and Jill fell down a hill and there's the issue of a broken crown. I must speak with the doctors and the reporters waiting at the hospital for the scoop (there's gossip that it wasn't an accident and Jill is to blame, but I will defend her). I may be gone for the next two days, and I fear I will not be back in time for the horse races. I know you are hexcited to attend. Perhaps you can bring Ooglot?

I recall your friend with the red cape invited you to her castle. If you want to make other plans for your Spring Break, I do understand.

Love,

Father

Tears stung Raven's eyes as she read the letter. She didn't want to go to the Princes race with Ooglot! She didn't want to eat a pizza! She wanted to spend quality time with her father. This was so fairy unfair! Before she could stop herself, her hurt and anger swirled together and jagged sparks exploded from her fingertips. The delicate china plate in front of her shattered into hundreds of tiny pieces.

Raven and Cook gasped together.

"I'm so sorry. I didn't mean for that to happen." Raven tried to gather the pieces. "I can fix it."

"Don't be upset. It's only a plate." Cook placed her hand warmly on Raven's shoulder. "And there's still a delicious dinner to eat," she added with a smile.

"Thanks, but I'm not feeling hungry right now. I'll just grab something later. Can you share the meal with the staff and everyone else so all that spelltacular food doesn't go to waste?"

Raven couldn't bear to eat the meal without her father, and she really had lost her appetite. Something was definitely off about her—she felt the same strange sensation she had been feeling on and off all day. She'd never been this quick to get angry, and she had never let her anger take control. She stared at her fingers. What was happening? Was her mother right?

"Home usually makes me feel more like me, but now I feel less like me. Do you know what I mean?" Raven asked Cook.

"Not really." Cook sighed. "But maybe you need a break from your Spring Break."

Raven's eyes widened. "Maybe you're right! It's time for a rewrite. Thanks for everything, Cook."

After Cook headed back into the kitchen, Raven pulled her MirrorPhone from her pocket and dialed Cerise. Her friend's face appeared on the screen. Maddie squeezed in next to her. Before they had the chance to even say hello, Raven burst out, "Still have room for me?"

The music of the three enchanted fiddles was drowned out by her friends' cheers. And in that moment, Raven felt like herself again for the first time all day.

Diary Entry

Other people's houses smell different,
Diary. I don't know what our castle smells
like, but Cerise's cozy cottage smells like
warm cinnamon buns and pine trees.

As soon as I emerged from the well (well
travel is the easiest way to reach the Dark
Forest), Red Riding Hood flung open the front
door and squeezed me in a tight, welcoming
hug, making me feel instantly at home.

I felt a pang of worry that I was going to cause problems for them just by being there. A visit from the daughter of the Evil Queen could cause a stir in the forest. But I pushed that thought to the back of my mind. I was invited! They wanted me here!

When I entered, Cerise smiled widely. Maddie turned three cartwheels in a row! Then Red handed me a basket of baked treats and suddenly my appetite returned. I ate three pecan tarts. Mr. Badwolf walked in as I was finishing and made a joke about me wolfing down the tarts. I didn't know what to do or say. I glanced nervously at Maddie. Had Cerise told her that Mr. Badwolf was her father?

As if he was trying to smooth over the awkward moment, Mr. Badwolf made another joke. "Wolf got your tongue?" he asked me.

Maddie peered into my mouth, and declared that my tongue was indeed there. Then she asked how a bandersnatch's bill is like a mushroom wearing boots, and we all cracked up laughing. You can always count on Maddie to make an awkward moment better.

As discreetly as I could, I asked Cerise if Maddie knew about her parents, but of course Maddie heard me and announced, for everyone to hear, that of course she knew. The Narrators had told her.

I'm so glad that Cerise and her parents don't have to keep this secret while we visit. As it is, they must keep the curtains shut at all times. Most people don't understand or approve of off-story romances.

I looked around for Ramona, Cerise's sister. Ramona goes to school with us, but I don't know her that well. It turns out she was spending the break with one of her friends.

Right now, Diary, I am tucked under a patchwork quilt in a huge wooden bed. Cerise is fast asleep and snoring loudly on my right side. Maddie is sleeping on my left side with her feet on the pillow and her head under the covers, and she's laughing as she dreams.

I am _so happy_ here with my BFFAs.

I'm sure I'll feel like myself tomorrow.

Spell you later,

Raven

Chapter 4

Tat-a-tat-tat-tat. The drumming of a wood-pecker's beak on a nearby tree trunk woke Raven with a start. What a strange sound! At home, the cries of the seagulls soaring over the cliffs trumpeted the sun-rise. At Ever After High, the sweet song of Apple's bluebirds started the day. It took Raven a moment to remember that she was in the Dark Forest.

She opened her eyes and saw two feet in fuzzy pink striped socks. They weren't standing on the floor. Instead, they waved in the air in time with the woodpecker's rhythmic beat.

Raven smiled. If Maddie's feet were up, that meant Maddie's head was down. Raven peeked over the edge of the bed.

"Hi, Raven," Maddie said from her spot on the floor. "A good morning stretch is a tea-rrific way to start the day. Tea is also a tea-rrific way to start the day, all day, every day." She turned rightside up. "I think it's time for my third tea party of the day."

Raven lazily rubbed her eyes and smiled at Maddie. She was used to Maddie's boundless energy, even first thing in the morning. "Hi, Cerise," she added, smiling at her other friend.

Cerise stood in front of her mirror, brushing her thick, white-streaked black hair. "I'm glad you're awake. You know how you said last night that you didn't have a good start to your vacation? I declare today a Day of Fun. Let's spellebrate that you're here!"

Raven bolted upright, suddenly energized. "What's first?"

"A picnic in the woods. My mom is already preparing a basket," Cerise said with a huge grin on her face.

At school, Cerise usually stayed quiet, hiding in the back of class so she wouldn't be noticed. Now, in her own home, Cerise's bright and bubbly personality was able to shine. Raven wished her friend could feel this way everywhere.

A little while later, the three girls set off into the forest to search for the perfect picnic spot. Maddie wandered ahead while Raven and Cerise traded opinions. Raven thought they should find a sunny, grassy hill to lay the plaid flannel blanket. Cerise wanted to tuck away under the shady canopy of intertwined branches.

"How about right here?" Maddie asked, appearing out of nowhere and plopping down in the middle of the ground. She patted the ground next to her, and Raven sat. Maddie gave her a peculiar, questioning sniff. Then she spotted an enormous oak tree and scrambled to her feet.

Maddie hexpertly climbed the tree to the highest branch. "I have a bird's-eye view of you. Except I'm using my own eye. We should picnic up here!" she called to her friends.

Raven and Cerise shared amused glances. Leave it to Maddie to find the most impossible picnic spot!

"We can't get a blanket up there," Raven called. "Even the birds don't build their nests that high."

"Fiddle-faddle!" Maddie held her nose and, before Raven could cry out in alarm, jumped off the branch, turned a somersault in the air, and landed smoothly on both feet. Then Maddie pushed up the sleeve of Raven's purple top and ran her fingers down Raven's bare arm.

"That tickles!" Raven said, squirming.

"Your skin is strangely rough...almost bumpy." Maddie held on to Raven hands and peered at her fingernails. "Your thumbnails have gotten long."

"Maddie, my skin is fine."

Cerise gave her friends a curious look. Just then, her stomach let out a very loud rumble. "I'm hungry! I know a picnic spot. Follow me." Cerise led them to a clearing.

Pine needles covered the cool forest floor, and velvety, emerald-green moss grew on smooth rocks.

"This spot is spelltacular," Raven said as she helped Cerise lay out the blanket for their picnic. She plopped down, ready to dig in to the delicious basket Red had packed for them, when she felt a peculiar sensation in her ear.

"Maddie! Why was your finger in my ear?" Raven demanded.

"I was measuring the hexact temperature of your earwax."

"What-ever-after for?"

"You're different today. Have you changed the direction that you brush your teeth? No? Are your leggings new? Is the royal purple more of a dark-magenta-mccts-fig?" Maddie scrunched up her face. "You seem... I don't know... Wonderlandian."

"I do? Is that good?"

"Wonderlandian is tea-rrific, but you seem off-center, topsy-turvy, quite crooked." Maddie gave Raven another big sniff. "I smell soap, but something dark and mysterious lurks underneath. Have you been under any bridges?"

"Do you smell this?" Cerise pulled a small spray bottle from the pocket of her cloak. She gave a spritz and the air clouded with the scent of garlic, cloves, and castor oil. "It's my mom's homemade bug repellent."

"Tea-rrifically stinky! That's it!" Maddie spun in a circle. "Or not. Who's to say? Only the nose knows."

Raven's stomach tightened, and the weird feeling she'd been getting at home settled over her, leaving her with a now-familiar fluttery feeling in her stomach. Her mother had said that evil would bloom in her. Was it starting now? Is that what Maddie smelled? Raven shivered at the horrible thought.

"I'm off to the Hood bakery," Mr. Badwolf called out as he strode into the clearing holding a wicker basket. "Red has been a pie-making machine. We're giving away the hextras. Anyone up for a pie run?"

"Please don't take all my helpers," Red said, hurrying up behind him. "I need the food from the kitchen brought outside. Anyone want to lend a hand?"

"Between all of us there are eight hands, and that's seven more than you need to brew a pot of charmberry tea!" Maddie declared.

Cerise laughed. "Mom, I think that means Maddie would love to help."

"I'll help deliver the pies," Raven offered. A walk in the woods would clear her head. She wanted to stop thinking about evil sprouting like a beanstalk inside her. She followed Mr. Badwolf into the trees as Maddie and Cerise returned to the cottage with Red.

Raven panted as she worked to keep pace with him. Thorny bushes snagged her purple skirt. Twigs cracked and leaves rustled under her black patent-leather high-tops. She was amazed by just how quickly and quietly Mr. Badwolf moved.

He finally stopped by a tree filled with ripe orange-red persimmons. The tomato-like fruit glistened in the sun. "Where are we?" asked Raven, surprised to see little cottages ahead. Red's cottage was nestled far, far away so they could live in peace.

"Hood Hollow," said Mr. Badwolf. "These are Red's people, before they turned on her. They're not my biggest fans."

"They're not mine, either." The last time Raven had visited, the Hoods had taunted and jeered her for being the daughter of the Evil Queen.

All of a sudden, Mr. Badwolf lifted his head and sniffed the air. He stroked his heavy beard and his nose twitched. Then he grabbed Raven's upper arm and yanked her behind the thick trunk of a nearby evergreen.

"Stay close," he whispered before darting behind another tall tree. Stealthily, he wove from tree to tree. Raven concentrated on staying right behind Mr. Badwolf.

"You're a natural at this," he added quietly.

"What is this? Is it a game?" asked Raven.

"You could say that. Keep out of sight," he warned. Then he was off again.

Raven followed, pleased that she could keep up. It was only when he scurried toward one of the Hood cottages that she hesitated. She watched in frozen fascination as he snatched a steaming pie cooling on the windowsill and tucked it into his wicker basket before darting away.

He ran toward another cottage. A pie also cooled on the windowsill, and he swiped this one as well.

Raven gulped as she realized what she was seeing. Mr. Badwolf was stealing the Hoods' pies! This wasn't a game. It was royally rotten and wrong.

She ran over to him in a huff. "Mr. Badwolf, we need to put them back," Raven said insistently.

She opened the basket and reached for the top two pies. Their spicy persimmon filling smelled delicious.

"No!" he growled. "They can't have these pies."

Raven didn't listen. All she could think about was giving back the stolen pies. She raced as fast as she could to the first cottage. She heard Hoods moving around inside. Mr. Badwolf was coming up behind her. Her heart pounded as she stared at the two pies in her hands. Which one had come from this windowsill?

She randomly chose one, balanced it on the sill, then raced to return the other to the second cottage. Back in the shadows of the tall trees, she bent over and fought to catch her breath.

"Normally, I'd applaud your evil, Raven." Mr. Badwolf towered over her. Somehow, he once again held the two pies. "I understand that the Hoods are no friends of ours, but at times, we must rein in our dark desires. Your mother crossed that line, and look where she is." He spoke in a grave whisper.

"*You* stole those pies!" Raven pointed at him. "I was putting them back."

"The persimmons on the tree were glistening. They'd been contaminated by ogre sweat. When digested, an ogre's sweat causes painful, itchy blisters. I took the persimmon pies to protect the Hoods. They are Red's people, ever after all."

Raven blinked in surprise. Mr. Badwolf had wanted to *help* the Hoods, and she had returned the poison pies. She could've hurt the Hoods if they'd eaten them. Once again, she'd tried to do good but ended up with evil.

Or *almost* evil.

She breathed out a sigh of relief, as Mr. Badwolf stomped the pies under his large feet and buried the remains.

Diary Entry

I'm spelltacularly embarrassed! Because
Mr. Badwolf is a villain in his story, I
assumed that everything he does must
be evil. I shouldn't judge people by labels.
We're not one-dimensional characters. Of all
people, I should know that!

Luckily, Mr. Badwolf was chill about
my mistake. And as we walked back from
delivering Red's hextra pies to the bakery,

he clapped me on the back and happily congratulated me on my final assignment.

I got an A!

(Wow! It's a good thing I found my thronework and handed it in.)

I did a happy dance right in front of my teacher. Crazy, right? But good grades are fairy important to me. Mr. Badwolf laughed. He liked that I was psyched about doing well in General Villainy class, which has never been one of my favorite subjects. He's sure my grades will continue to improve if I work hard. Then he called me "a natural" at General Villainy. He said I was Born To Be Evil.

I stopped dancing. My mood darkened.

I want to hand back that A. I want him to give me a much worse grade, because then I won't have to wonder if my mother has been right.

Mr. Badwolf noticed the change in my mood. He told me on the way back to the picnic that I've gone sinisterly sullen, that mood swings are a curse all villains endure!

I explained that I'm just conflicted. I want to do well in his class, but at the same time, I don't. Something is happening inside me...or maybe it's not....Sometimes I get angry....I want to do good, but then it gets messed up....

My words became all jumbled when I tried to explain. Maddie's Riddlish makes more sense than I was making!

Guess what he thought my babble meant. Are you ready?

He thought I was confiding that <u>I was evil ever after all!</u>

He actually howled with joy.

Ugh! Total disconnect.

Then—here comes the thorny part—he said he hexpects I'll hexcell at exploring my evil destiny in General Villainy next semester.

<u>I DO NOT WANT TO EXPLORE MY EVIL DESTINY!!!!!!</u>

Spell you later,

Raven

Chapter 5

"Wild and woodsy tea party time!" cried Maddie when Raven returned to the picnic blanket. Mr. Badwolf had walked on to the cottage to help Red carry the last of the food. Raven tucked her legs under her as she sat between Maddie and Cerise.

Today, Maddie's hat looked like a bird's nest woven out of pink cotton candy. She reached inside the spun sugar and pulled out five teacups in a pale robin's-egg blue. Then she pulled out tiny spoons and a matching teapot.

"The tea is a special blend of grass and bark with a hint of soil." Maddie took a sip. "It needs a splash of dandelion wish."

She cartwheeled over to a sunny patch of grass and plucked a dandelion. The once-yellow weed had dried into a white ball of fluffy seeds. Opening the teapot lid, she closed her eyes and blew in all the seeds. *Dandelion puff and stuff, sends wonders and wishes,"* she sang.

"What in Ever After are you doing?" asked Cerise.

"In Wonderland, weeds bring wishes. Or is it fishes? I can never remember. Wait, the plural of fish isn't fishes. It's fish." She smelled the tea. "Oh good. It isn't fishy. It's wish-licious!"

Raven laughed. Maddie always made her forget her troubles.

"Look what else I have!" Maddie pulled a cherry-red teapot trimmed with a black-and-white checkerboard design from her hat. A red ribbon tied into a bow topped the pot.

"So fairy fancy!" exclaimed Raven.

"My father picked it out as a thank-you gift for Red and Mr. Badwolf for having me at their home. He always finds the most perfect pots." Maddie looked around. "Should we sip, or does a hat-tastic hostess wait for all her guests?"

"I feel so bad! I was in such a rush to get here that I forgot to bring a present." Raven bit her lip. In truth, her father hadn't been around to remind her, and her mother had never once given a gift as an expression of gratitude. The Evil Queen hexpected presents bestowed upon her, not the other way around.

"Don't worry about it, Raven," said Cerise. "You guys being here is the best present of all. We never-ever-after have visitors." Cerise stood and headed to the cottage. "I'm going to find them before the tea turns cold."

Maddie nestled close to the teapot. "I'll keep it toasty until you return."

"I really want to give them a present, too," Raven confided once Cerise was out of earshot.

"That calls for a shopping spree-a-dee!" Maddie squealed. "Do squirrels have stores? Is there an underground mole mall?"

"I doubt it." Raven's shoulders slumped as she surveyed the miles and miles of trees. "I don't think there's anything to buy here."

"Presents don't need to cost money. Weave a blanket from spiderwebs. Catch a rainbow in a glass jar. Write a poem on a leapin' lily pad."

"You're onto something." Raven looked around, taking in all the options. "Those chipmunks' cheeks are filled with nuts. How about a platter of mixed nuts? Maybe the chipmunks will share."

"Toadstools! Sharing is caring," agreed Maddie.

Raven knelt on the ground, waving the cute chipmunks over. They looked like the adorable woodland creatures that followed Apple White everywhere and happily did everything she asked. They even cleaned her room!

"Hi there. I'm Raven Queen and I wanted to talk to you about—"

"Ah!" The chipmunks gave a startled cry at the sound of her name. In a horrified rush, they scurried away as fast as their little legs could carry them.

"How royally rude!" Maddie shook her head.

Raven sighed. "It happens. Woodland creatures fear me. It's the whole daughter-of-the-Evil-Queen reputation. What else can I find?"

Raven searched behind a row of holly bushes. She spotted a polka-dot ruffle mushroom, but what if it was poisonous? She tried to leap for a platinum moth, but it soared too high. Then a sparkle of blue growing by a fallen tree branch caught her eye. She leaned down and sucked in her breath.

The itty-bitty flower's shimmery purple petals were as sheer as fairy wings.

"Raven, where are you? We're all back and there's tons of food," called Cerise.

"Teatime!" called Maddie.

Raven stared at the minuscule flower. Would Red and Mr. Badwolf appreciate its petite beauty? She thought of him holding it in his large, paw-like hands. He'd crush it. Hex no! She couldn't give them such a tiny present.

If only it were larger and more impressive looking. If it were the size of a sunflower, that would really be something memorable.

Raven sighed. A flower couldn't grow in a few minutes.

Unless...no! So far her magic spells had all had disastrous results.

She gently plucked the delicate flower from the earth and cupped it inside both palms. She decided there was no need to risk a spell backfiring in an attempt to make it bigger. She'd give it just as nature had grown it.

"There you are, dear. Can I make you a plate?" Red's warm voice welcomed her as she returned to the blanket.

Raven's eyes widened at the feast—there were jamberry sandwiches, watermelon-radish salad, beet soup, cherry pie, and Red-velvet cake. Everything was red! Mr. Badwolf poured tea, using the new red teapot.

Raven glanced down at her cupped hands. Suddenly, she regretted her decision not to make the flower larger. She needed a more impressive gift to show how happy she was to be here. She wanted this flower to be as big as the gratitude she felt.

Raven pushed her palms together, and a small explosion of magical sparks surrounded the tiny flower.

Diary Entry

Curses! It happened again. My magic backfired! I'll tell you the details, but be warned: It's beyond cringeworthy.

So I give this long speech thanking Red Riding Hood, Mr. Badwolf, and Cerise for inviting me, and I say I have a present for them. All this time, I feel tingling inside my cupped hands, almost like tiny pinpricks, but I figure it's the aftereffects of the magic.

I dramatically open my hands. Now I'm hexpecting an enormous purple flower to spring up and for Red to gasp in delight. Instead, <u>ants</u> crawl from my palms. I'm not talking a few ants. Dozens—maybe hundreds—of ants invade the picnic!

Once again, dark magic + good intentions = catastrophe. What is wrong with me????

There's an army of ants <u>everywhere</u>: in Red's food, in Mr. Badwolf's long hair, in the folds of Cerise's cape, in Maddie's nest-hat! I'm waiting for Red to cry out in horror, but she surprises me and says, "Ants at a picnic—how perfect! You're so thoughtful to bring them in my favorite color, too."

Do you know what kind of ants are red, Diary? <u>FIRE-BREATHING ANTS!</u>

I had no idea what to do. I froze like a griffin in headlights. What a disaster!

Maddie to the rescue! With her face squished against the blanket, Maddie welcomed every last ant to the picnic. Then she pulled a tiny teapot from her hat for an ant-tastic tea party. She led the ants far, far away from our picnic and poured each an itsy-bitsy cup of super-sugary tea (ants love sweets).

I ♡ my friends!!!!

But seriously, what is going on with my magic and all these fairy-fails?

Spell you later,

Raven

Chapter 6

Crumbs sprayed from Mr. Badwolf's mouth, and he slurped loudly as he lapped up the tea. Raven realized that if she didn't chew faster, Mr. Badwolf would wolf down all the delicious pie and cake before she made it to dessert. Raven imagined the disapproving glare her mother would give if she were at their picnic. The Evil Queen had always taught her daughter, "It is okay to do bad things, but there's no excuse for bad manners."

Raven gave Mr. Badwolf a pass. He *was*, after all, part wolf.

After the last little morsel was polished off, he yawned. "How about a stroll through the woods as our meal settles?" he asked Red.

"We'll be back soon, girls," Red said as they walked toward the woods.

Cerise stood and stretched her lean calf muscles. "Anyone for a race through the woods?"

"Sure, I'll give it a try," said Raven. Cerise was the star of their school's Track and Shield, so Raven knew she probably wouldn't be able to keep up, but she didn't care about winning. She was happy to run for fun.

"I'll hop," Maddie said. "Shall I wear my tap shoes?"

"I don't think they'll make noise on the dirt." Cerise pointed out the path that led through the trees to a finish vine at the top of a hill.

"Well, then, there's no point in hopping with both feet," Maddie said cheerfully. "I'll start you. Ready? On your mark, don't sleep like a sloth, a loose goose will vamoose!"

"Go?" Raven and Cerise asked, both unsure how to translate the Riddlish.

"Yes!" cried Maddie.

Cerise and Raven took off. Maddie hopped on one foot and was quickly left in their dust. She laughed merrily as she scampered with a squirrel. She was in no rush to reach the finish vine.

But Cerise was. Her powerful legs surged her forward. Her red cloak flapped as she darted around trees, pivoting into the turns.

Raven worked hard to stay behind her friend, keeping time with the soft thuds of Cerise's brown boots. Cool air filled her lungs, and the heavy weight that had settled into her stomach since the start of Spring Break began to dissolve. The faster she ran, the happier she felt—as if she could outrun the odd feeling that had mysteriously invaded her body.

Raven increased her speed. Soon, she was running alongside Cerise. This was spelltacular. Her heart hammered in her chest and her breathing was ragged as she set her gaze on the finish vine.

I can win this.

The thought almost stopped her in her tracks. What story did she think she was in? She could never-ever-after beat super-athletic Cerise.

This race isn't fair. Raven debated whether she should quit. Cerise was half wolf! She wasn't even panting.

No! I'm not a quitter. I can run faster. I want to win!

Raven pumped her legs harder. Sweat trickled down her forehead. They were neck and neck.

Am I being mean?

Raven worried that it was bad-spirited to want to beat Cerise. This run was supposed to be for fun.

It's more fun to win.

Competing voices filled Raven's thoughts. No longer paying attention to the race, she tried to untangle her conflicting feelings.

Ooof! Cerise suddenly stumbled. Raven looked back and saw her friend get right back on her feet, so feeling confident Cerise wasn't hurt, she sprinted forward as fast as she could and crossed the finish vine first.

"Woo-hoo! I won!" Raven waved her arms in victory.

"Congrats!" Cerise wrapped her in a sincere hug. "That was a hexcellent run!"

"Great job, girls!" Mr. Badwolf crouched on a large rock. Raven hadn't realized he'd gotten back from his walk and had watched the race. He ambled over and clapped both girls on the back. "Cerise, great speed as always. Raven, that was quite a performance."

Raven grinned. "This is the first running race I've won since nursery-rhyme school. I didn't think I had it in me to run so fast!"

"Raven!" Mr. Badwolf guffawed. "Your speed alone didn't bring victory. You remind me so much of your mother as a girl. We went to school together, you know that? Win by any means necessary. That was your mother's motto, too. Take down the competition. Trip 'em, if you have to! That's the true mark of an evil winner!"

Raven replayed the race in her mind. What had she been doing when Cerise stumbled? She couldn't remember. She'd been trying to quell her dark thoughts. Had she done something bad to win? Had she *tripped* Cerise?

"Who won?" Maddie hopped toward them.

The weight in Raven's stomach grew heavier. What should she do?

She took off running. She wanted that happy feeling to return.

"Raven! Come back!" her friends called.

She plunged even deeper into the woods, running as fast as she could.

But there was no outrunning her destiny.

She was turning evil after all.

Diary Entry

I'm sitting under a little wooden bridge. It's dark and quiet down here next to the shallow stream. I'm sitting here and trying to sort this all out.

All signs point to me being evil.

1. Every good spell I've done has gone bad.

2. I almost let the Hoods eat poisoned pie.

3. I tripped my BFFA and
  sabotaged our race.

But I still feel <u>good</u> inside. How's that
even possible? Can I be a good person and
sometimes do wicked things or have wicked
thoughts? What if I can't stop what-ever-after
is happening and I become pure villain?

I can't even go there. I'd give anything not to
be evil. I'll never eat another thronecake again.
I'll live the rest of my life under this bridge!

Actually, it's not so bad down here. A
little damp, maybe. That's so weird. Why
am I thinking about living under a bridge?

Cerise and Maddie found me here
after I ran away. Cerise tracked me with
that super-sniffer of hers. Now they're
patiently waiting for me to finish up

writing in you. They know I need to get my crown on straight!

I told Cerise how bad I felt that I had tripped her. Cerise told me not to worry about it, that she'd bumped her knee the other day and had been feeling a little wobbly, so it probably wasn't even my fault. So that explains why I was even able to keep up with her, but, Diary, what if I really did trip her?

I told my friends that I was worried I might really be evil and that I've been feeling confused about my destiny.

Then Maddie pointed out that I've been confused about that ever since my first day at Ever After High.

She's got me there, Diary.

I tried to explain that this was
different. That I had this weird feeling.
Maddie and Cerise listened (they are such
great friends!) and Maddie even had some
advice for me. She told me that everything
made perfect Wonderlandian sense to her:
I'd done a double backflip back because
I'd taken a huge leap forward on Legacy
Day, and now I had to front flip back
over to the side of good.

In other words, according to Maddie, I
have to do a front-flip-full-twist.

A front-flip-full-twist? Is she serious?

I can barely do a cartwheel.

I'm doomed.

Spell you later,
Raven

Chapter 7

I know you keep saying nothing is impossible," Raven told Maddie. "But, trust me, I royally stink at gymnastics."

"When I couldn't do the hurdles in Track and Shield, I practiced and practiced until I conquered it," offered Cerise. "You can just practice the front-flip-full-twist."

"I could...." Raven thought about what Maddie had said earlier. She needed to get back to the side of good. A smile slowly spread across her face as she formulated her plan. "I have another way. From now on, I'm going to do only good things. I'm going to be so off-the-script good that I'll conquer any eviltude that tries to come my way."

"In Wonderland, we like to play If I Didn't while enjoying a pot of jubjub tea!" Maddie did her own flip. "In other words, good triumphs over evil in The End."

"Problem solved." Cerise stood, knocking her head against the wooden planks. "Can we get out from under this bridge now?"

"Why are you under a bridge, anyway?" asked Maddie.

Raven shrugged. "I have absolutely no idea. It just seemed like a nice place to hide out and think."

On the way back to the cottage, Raven complimented her friends. She picked up the litter left behind from their picnic. She gathered nuts for the chipmunks. She focused on doing good, good, good. When she spotted the plump, ripe raspberries on the bushes near the cottage, she knew what to do.

"These berries are the perfect gift for Red to make up for the ants. We can make berry jam!" Raven said excitedly, before realizing she didn't know how.

Raven turned to Maddie. "I've never made jam before," she admitted.

"*Ooh*, tea-rrific! There's a first time for everything! And a third, sixth, and eighth!" Maddie declared.

The three girls lifted the hems of their dresses, piling on berries until the fabric sagged under their weight.

"My mom mushes berries with a wooden spoon in a bowl to make jam. We're going to need a lot of bowls. Or"—Cerise pointed to an empty wheelbarrow near their vegetable garden—"what about one ginormous bowl?"

"Hex yeah!" cried Raven. They dumped all the berries into the wheelbarrow. "Should I go inside to get spoons?"

"Spoons are so last chapter. Today is totally about toes!" Maddie pulled off her mismatched shoes and socks, rinsed her bare feet with the garden hose, and climbed into the wheelbarrow.

"Have you flipped your crown?" Cerise gripped the handles to steady the wheelbarrow so her friend wouldn't fall.

Raven pulled off her socks and shoes, rinsed her feet, and scampered up beside Maddie. The berries felt cold and gloppy between her toes. They held hands and danced until the fruit was pulverized into a pulpy sauce.

"Next we cook it with sugar on the stove."

Cerise seemed surprised by how much she'd picked up from all those afternoons at the kitchen table, watching her mother cook. "Jump out. I've got this."

Cerise helped her friends out and rolled the wheelbarrow through the back door and into the kitchen.

"I want to cook, too!" Raven hurried in behind her. She paused for just a moment, remembering her last adventure in a kitchen. She quickly pushed that thought to the back of her mind and rushed into the kitchen. From now on, she would only do good!

"Jumpin' jelly donuts!" Maddie stood in the doorway and clapped her hands over her mouth. "Look what you did, Raven."

Bright-red berry-juice footprints covered the floor, staining the polished wood. Raven had forgotten to put her shoes back on.

"Ugh! My good is turning all big bad again." Raven couldn't believe it. She'd tried so hard. "Don't worry, Cerise. I'll clean it before your mom gets back."

Raven wiggled her fingers at the floor, ready to spark some magic. Then she balled her hands into tight fists. She'd tried that path already. Magic wasn't going to get her back on the side of good. She turned to the sink. "I'm going old-school this time—a sponge, a mop, and lots of soap."

When Red entered later, she was met with two surprises: a shiny, clean kitchen and jars of delicious, homemade raspberry jam.

In the cozy kitchen, they gathered around the small table. Raven sat back in her chair, enjoying the warmth from the nearby fireplace and the laughter as Maddie delighted them with stories and riddles. Raven watched

Cerise and Mr. Badwolf's teeth flash as they chewed their meat vigorously, both leaning with their elbows on the table and both talking with food in their mouths. She laughed as Red and Cerise both trustingly fell for Mr. Badwolf's trickery and smiled as both took special care to refill her water glass and offer second helpings.

It dawned on her how much Cerise had inherited from both her parents, in looks and personality.

"I baked a fairytale desert for each of you," Red announced after the girls had helped clear the dinner plates. "Mini-thronecakes. Cerise's is cherry flavored. Raven's is dark chocolate. Maddie's is a pineapple upside-down."

"Can I eat it upside down?" Maddie balanced her head on the seat of the chair and raised her legs in the air.

"Eat any way you want. It's my mother's recipe. She used to bake mini-thronecakes for me to bring to my grandma."

"And we all know how that story turns out!" Mr. Badwolf gave Red a mischievous nudge. "I guarantee these thronecakes are the most spelltacular ones you've ever tasted!"

"I had the most marvelous thronecake the day we left school for Spring Break." Raven reached for her fork. "I don't know what flavor it was. It tasted like all my favorite foods rolled into one. Isn't that hexcellent? But it did make me feel woozy and dizzy when I ate it. Probably too much sugar."

"Really?" Mr. Badwolf's ears perked up. "Who gave you that thronecake?"

"Maddie, I think." Raven turned to her friend. "Curses! I didn't say thank you."

"Don't thank me. It wasn't from me."

"Then it must've been Apple. A little white box was on my bed when I got back from the Castleteria," Raven reported.

Maddie flipped to her feet. "Wait a spell. Something is topsy-turvy. I saw Faybelle right outside your room that day, and she was holding a little white box."

"Faybelle?" That didn't make any sense. "Why would she give me a secret thronecake?"

Diary Entry

"The thronecake may have been cursed."

Did you hear that, Diary? Cursed! That's what Mr. Badwolf said—and if anyone knows about curses, it's him. He teaches General Villainy!

I excused myself from the table to go to the bathroom. I needed a minute to think this through.

Why would Faybelle want to curse me?

Sure, we're not BFFAs, but we're not enemies, either. I know she's against my choice to not follow my destiny, but unlike others, Faybelle has told me outright. I respect her honesty. I figure that she chose her story, I'm writing a new one, and everything's cool.

Maybe it's not.

What I don't get is: Why does she care so much? My choice only affects me, Apple, and—I guess—my mother.

Oh hello!

Now it's all adding up.

A cursed thronecake has the Evil Queen's fingerprints all over it. And the little card that said EAT ME! I remember cards like that in my nursery-rhyme school snack bag.

My mother and Faybelle are working <u>together</u> to curse me.

Was it a curse to turn me wicked? Is that what my mother was talking about during our mirror chat? Is that why all my good is going bad? Can the curse be reversed?

I hope so!!!!!!

I have so many questions, Diary.

Fingers crossed that Mr. Badwolf has answers.

Spell you later,
Raven

Chapter 8

Raven returned to the table and poked her thronecake with her fork. Molten fudge seeped from the moist dark chocolate cake, but she couldn't bring herself to take a bite. Had Faybelle ruined thronecake for her forever after?

"How difficult would it be to curse a thronecake?" she asked Mr. Badwolf.

"It depends on the difficulty of the curse. My friends and I once cursed a milk shake back in our day at Ever After High. Made our teacher croak like a frog uncontrollably whenever a student raised her hand—and the kids in that class asked a lot of questions!"

"But is there a curse that would make me evil that could be done to a thronecake?" Raven asked.

"Make *you* evil?" He raised his bushy eyebrows. "You were born evil."

Raven sucked her breath in through her teeth. "I don't think I was. I know my mother is the ultimate evil, but I'm not like her. At least I thought I wasn't, but since I ate that thronecake, I've been feeling, well, grumpy, mixed-up, and a little bit evil."

"And she smells weird, too," Maddie added. "Like a mixture of broccoli and old coffee."

"Seriously?" Raven was even more horrified. She was jumping into a shower right after dinner!

"You don't say." Mr. Badwolf pressed his fingers together. "That changes things."

"What does it change?" asked Cerise.

"There's an obscure curse I know of, designed to ignite evil, but it only works fully if the recipient possesses true evil in her core. The thing is, this curse is meant to be used on...well...*trolls.*"

"No worries, then. Raven is not evil, and she's not a troll," Red concluded.

"Trolls often smell like broccoli and old coffee, in my experience," Mr. Badwolf informed them.

"Whoa!" Raven jumped out of her chair. "Are you saying I've been turned evil *and* into a troll?"

For a moment, the room began to spin. Raven gripped the back of the chair to steady herself. How much was one princess supposed to take? She had planned on kicking back this week—so much for a relaxing Spring Break!

"Don't worry!" Maddie patted her hand. "You don't look like a troll. You just smell like one."

"Oh great. Troll odor!" Raven sighed.

"But she was sitting under the bridge," Cerise whispered to Maddie. "She had bugs in her hands, and she's been grumpy."

"That's not proof. I once almost caught a fly with my tongue, but that doesn't make me a frog," Maddie whispered back.

"Um, hello? I can hear you," Raven reminded her friends.

"I doubt anything is happening," said Mr. Badwolf. "That curse is in an old book that is hidden safely away in the Vault of Lost Tales. No one can get that book."

"See?" Red smiled. "It's just a coincidence."

"When you say *no one*, does that include the Evil Queen?" Raven asked warily.

"The Evil Queen?" Mr. Badwolf snarled. "Well, she's the hexception. The Evil Queen finds ways to get what she desires."

"Well, she *desires* for me to be evil just like she is," Raven replied, collapsing into the chair again and hiding her face in her hands. She didn't like the way this was coming together.

"But you're not evil!" cried Cerise. "You're not cursed. This is crazy."

"I hope I am cursed, because then I'd know what was going on. Otherwise, I'm becoming who I was born to be. What if I can't choose my own destiny ever after all?"

"You *can* write your own story," Cerise insisted. "My parents did it, and look at our happy family."

"You have the best family, Cerise," Raven agreed. "My family, well, we're much more complicated."

Cerise snorted. "You don't think my family is complicated?"

"Everyone's family is complicated in their own way. That's what makes life interesting," added Red.

"I wouldn't trade my family for the world. I like being sweet like my mom and wild like my dad. I like that my parents chose love instead of following storybook rules." Cerise wrapped Mr. Badwolf and Red in a hug.

Raven was overcome with longing to hug her father. "I miss my dad," she admitted.

"You should talk to him," suggested Mr. Badwolf.

"He's so busy." Raven swallowed hard. "He doesn't have time to listen."

"Have you told him you *really* need to talk to him?" asked Maddie.

"The Good King solves all the kingdom's problems, right? He'll know if it's your fate or if it's a curse. It's your turn now," encouraged Cerise. "He's your dad, ever after all."

"You're right." Raven turned to Red, Mr. Badwolf, and Cerise. "My visit was super spelltacular, but would it be okay if I left a little early?"

Then Raven sent her dad a hext:

be home soon. rlly need 2 talk 2 u!!!!!
xoxo

Raven hurried to the well. Before she jumped in, she crossed her fingers and toes. Would the Good King be waiting when she got back to the castle?

Diary Entry

Home, sweet home!!!! Have you ever gone away, even for a short time, and then come home and crawled into your own bed with your own pillow? It's fableous!

Here's what happened....

Dad was waiting for me!!! Before I said anything, he gave me the <u>biggest</u> hug. Cook made us steaming mugs of hot chocolate, and we sat together in the great room in front of a roaring fire. I spilled my spells and told him underlineeverything.

He thought the idea of me becoming evil was Royally Ridiculous. He listed tons of good things I've done, like:

- When my mom's horse, Midnight, was sick, I sat in her stall and sang to her all night long.
- I always share my thronecakes, even though it's my favorite dessert (or at least it was...).

Dad reminded me that all kids are a mixture of both their parents. Some kids take after their mother more, some take after their father more, some kids have equal doses of both parents, and some are completely unique. I can't deny I have a bit of my mother in me, but Dad said I inherited her passion and her resolve—<u>not</u> her wicked ways.

I think he's right about that.

He said that good people make mistakes and sometimes do things they wish they hadn't, but that's okay. It's what's in my heart that counts. If I believe in myself one hundred percent, no evil spell can make me into something I'm not. Plus, in order for that curse to work, I would've had to be evil in my core. And that's so not me.

I am good.

I am <u>good</u>!

<u>I am good!</u>

Wow! I feel a zillion times better just writing it. From now on, I'm going to stay confident and not let others label me—even my mom.

Then I asked my dad to smell me. He was totally confused, but he did it.

"You smell like chocolate, well water, roses..." he said. "And broccoli."

Hex no! The curse didn't make me evil, but maybe it...

How do I get rid of the hextra helping of troll my mother served me?!

I was about to run to the mirror and confront her, but Dad asked if I still wanted to ride by his side at the races. If so, I needed to change into riding breeches and saddle up a horse pronto.

A no-brainer! Off to the races!

Oh...I almost forgot the best part. My dad apologized for being so busy. He hadn't realized how much I needed him. He told me that in the whole entire kingdom, I'm always #1 for him.

How great is that?

Spell you later,

Raven

Chapter 9

As four jet-black stallions pulled her royal carriage up to the front doors of Ever After High, Raven peered out the window, scanning the drop-off line for a certain familiar face. Ashlynn Ella stepped delicately out of her pumpkin carriage, wearing only one high-heeled shoe and the other foot bare. Daring Charming was in the middle of telling Dexter and Darling some long-winded story while they rolled their eyes and laughed. Holly O'Hair read a book under the large elm tree while Poppy O'Hair braided a strand of her hair. Their sunburned, freckled noses told Raven that the daughters of Rapunzel spent their Spring Break outside on their balcony.

But where was Faybelle?

More than ever after, Raven suspected she had traces of troll in her. This morning she'd noticed that her fingernails and toenails had the strangest greenish tinge to them now. She'd never been close enough to a troll to study their gnarled nails, but she was pretty sure they were green.

Raven stepped down, and Cedar Wood rushed over, eager to share stories about her boat trip with her father. But Raven's attention was soon drawn to syncopated clapping echoing from the courtyard. She excused herself to hurry over to the cheerhexers.

Welcome back! Hello!

Ready? (clap) Let's do it! (clap, clap)

On the final clap, she caught Faybelle's eye. "We need to talk."

"What-ever-after." Faybelle tightened her high ponytail. "Some privacy, please." The cheerhexers obeyed immediately, flying off in a line and pumping their fists in the air as if departing a bookball field at halftime.

Faybelle crossed her arms impatiently. "What's up, Raven?"

"*Hmm*, maybe that cursed thronecake you gave me?" Raven stood eye-to-eye with her.

"What thronecake?" Faybelle asked. She was playing innocent.

"Oh please. You've been helping the Evil Queen again! I don't know what you have up your wing, and I don't really care. You can make your own mistakes, but I don't want any part of it."

"News flash! Not everything revolves around you, Raven." Faybelle smirked.

"I know that, but when it comes to my mother, it seems to. She used you to get to me. We don't agree on a lot of things, but I've heard you in class and you're really smart. You deserve better than being my mother's messenger."

Faybelle blinked at the unhexpected compliment. Then she leaned close, so her upturned nose almost touched Raven's. "So, did you eat it?"

Raven nodded.

"It didn't work, did it? You still seem so *nice.* Or"—she clapped her hands over her mouth to control a sudden fit of giggles—"did you turn into a troll?"

"No!" Raven refused give Faybelle the satisfaction. Besides, she hadn't turned into a total troll, although she did yearn to crouch under the nearby table.

"A fairy can hope, can't she?" Faybelle sighed.

"Did you give the Evil Queen a book from the Vault of Lost Tales?" Raven asked.

"Maybe." Faybelle inspected her light-blue manicure, refusing to meet Raven's gaze. This was probably as close to a confession as Raven was going to get.

Faybelle shifted uncomfortably. "Listen, are you going to tell Headmaster Grimm that I sneaked up to the attic without permission and talked to the Evil Queen? Are you going to tell him about the cursed thronecake? I've been in trouble before. I think Headmaster Grimm will hexpel me this time."

As upset as Raven was with Faybelle, she didn't want her to be kicked out of school. "I won't say anything. But you should stop talking to my mother. Her dark power is stronger than you can even imagine. She's hextremely dangerous...even to you."

Faybelle gave the smallest nod, but Raven doubted she would follow her warning.

"Hey, Raven." Faybelle turned to leave. "Thanks."

Raven would have preferred a full-out apology, but she let it go. Faybelle was a supporting character in this play. She needed to confront the woman in the spotlight. She headed directly for Headmaster Grimm's office.

"Ms. Queen!" Headmaster Grimm adjusted his silk necktie and stood from his chair as she entered the wood-paneled room. "What brings you here?"

Raven didn't mention Faybelle.

"May I have permission to talk to my mother?" She worked to keep her voice light, as if this were a normal call home.

"Didn't you just come from your castle?"

"I did, but it was so busy." She began to describe the Princes Race in detail, down to the number of buttons on each prince's shirt. She knew Headmaster Grimm was a busy man with little patience.

"Fine, fine." He dipped his quill pen in blue ink and signed his name to a special pass. "Off you go. Be back in time for the assembly in the Charmitorium."

As Raven climbed the attic stairs, she concentrated on taking big gulps of air to slow her rapidly beating heart.

I've got this, she reminded herself.

The Evil Queen's curse had failed to turn

her wicked. Her mother couldn't make her be something she wasn't.

"I'm back!" Raven called out.

The Evil Queen materialized in the mirror. Her black velvet ball gown had tight sleeves that tapered to razor-sharp points on her hands. A thorny tiara rested on her dark hair, and her lips were painted blood-red. "I like the force of your greeting. No more of that wishy-washy stuff. You got me just before my party started. Granted, it's a party of one, since I'm all alone here. So, tell me... how was Spring Break? What deliciously dastardly deeds did you do?"

"It was really fun. I destroyed Cook's clean kitchen. I ruined Red's picnic with an army of fire-breathing ants. Oh, and I tripped Cerise to win a race!" Raven forced herself to sound hexcited.

"My girl!" The Queen's violet eyes blazed with delight. "Didn't I tell you how royally wonderful it is to embrace your wicked ways?"

"Now that I've started, I want to do more." Raven kept the smile plastered to her face. It was important for her mother to think her curse had worked. "Mr. Badwolf told me that the most terrifying curses aren't in our hextbooks. Can you believe they keep them locked away in the Vault of Lost Tales? There's one red book that has the worst spells, but"—she sighed for effect—"no one is powerful enough to get to that book."

The Evil Queen let out a long, loud cackle. "I am powerful enough!"

"But you're locked up. Oh well, it would've been so great if I could see that book. I'd love to, um, try some of those evil spells...."

"*Never* underestimate your mother. I have your precious book."

"Really?" Raven gasped in fake surprise.

"Of course," the Queen replied before disappearing momentarily. She returned, cradling the slim book in her hands. "Here it is—the darkest of the dark magic. What kind of spell shall we conjure together? What if we curse that brat Apple White with flaky foot fungus?"

"May I see the book?" Raven asked. "I'd like to choose the spell."

"Love that go-get-'em attitude!" The Evil Queen pushed the book against the mirror's glass. "Give me your hand, my evil darling daughter."

Raven's arm twitched, but she resisted reaching through. Breaking the mirror with her hand would set her mother free, and then terror would reign.

"Just toss me the book," Raven responded.

"If you are truly evil, you'll help me escape. We will rule together!"

Raven squared her shoulders and held her chin high. "I refuse to share. I am the future Evil Queen, so I decide when and how you escape from mirror prison, Mother. Throw me that book—*now*!"

The Queen didn't move.

Had Raven gone too far? Was she about to feel the Evil Queen's wrath?

Raven didn't need to worry. The Queen's heart swelled with pride. Her daughter *was* breathtakingly evil! The haughty tone and the sneering disdain had been pitch-perfect. She tossed the book to her daughter.

Raven scooped it off the dusty floor and flipped through the brittle, yellowed pages. *Merman Fins. Happiness Hiccups.*

Where was it?

Then she landed on *Evil Igniter.*

"Did you find something wicked?" Her mother craned her neck for a glimpse.

"Wicked, yes." Raven scowled and turned to the back of the book for the counter curse. "And that's what I came to fix."

She squinted at the tiny calligraphy. All she had to do was read the words while she put her index finger in her ear. She thought back on all the magic gone wrong. What if she messed this up, too? Would she get *more* troll-like?

The Evil Queen waited impatiently. The balance of power had shifted, and for the first time in a while, Raven felt in control and confident. Her belief in herself surpassed her mother's magic.

She poked her finger in her ear and recited:

> Redo, repeal, reverse,
> Overturn the curse.
> Evil begone, troll no more,
> Make me as I was before.

An electric tingle ricocheted from her eardrum to her toes and back again, causing shivers throughout her body. At the same time, a warm glow settled upon her.

She thought about bridges. Did she want to live under one? Hex no!

She thought about bugs. *Disgusting!*

All the troll-ness was gone!

Magic definitely worked better with confidence.

"I just reversed your curse," Raven boldly informed her mother. "If we're being honest here, it wasn't your best work. The evil part failed, because I'm not evil. And the curse was for trolls, which I certainly am not and never will be."

"What? B-b-but you did all those evil things. And you sounded so wicked."

"It was an act to trick you into giving me the book." Raven grinned. "You need to accept that I'm not destined to be like you. Now I'm going to do the right thing and return this horrid book to Giles Grimm. He will lock it up with a spell even you can't break, and you will never-ever-after recite another curse from it again."

Raven headed out of the attic and down the stairs, with the book of spells tucked safely under her arm. She didn't bother to say good-bye.

The Evil Queen watched her daughter depart. She wasn't as upset as she'd thought she'd be. Sure, the curse didn't work, but Raven was growing up and becoming more confident. Even the Evil Queen agreed—that was a *good* thing.

Diary Entry

I'm pretty impressed with myself. I reversed the curse <u>and</u> I've been writing in you every day, Diary. I'm pretty good at this diary thing. That reminds me....Where is the other journal? I need to fill in the spells I tried over Spring Break. Baba Yaga is going to have a lot to say about all my fairy-fails!

Guess who just walked into the room?

Apple!!!! She's back!

She returned with a hextra trunk filled with brand-new ruffled skirts, silky shirts, and beautiful red shoes. Apple was so busy unpacking and modeling her fancy fishtail braid that she didn't see my gift.

She was hexcited when she realized it was a jar of jam, but when she realized I'd actually made the jam, she was hextra hexcited...until I confessed that Maddie and I mushed the berries with our toes. Apple looked less hexcited about the jam until I remembered to tell her that we'd washed our feet. Then I showed her the photos on my MirrorPhone, and she quickly shared them with Briar Beauty and Darling Charming. They're already going viral.

Apple had a present for me, too.

She handed me a small white pastry
box.

One guess what was inside.

You got it—a <u>thronecake</u>!

I mean, really? Are we going there again?

Apple didn't understand when I
wouldn't eat it—after all, they used to
be my favorite. Apple and I have a <u>lot</u> of
catching up to do!

I'm putting you away now, Diary. I need
to tell Apple all about my week. And maybe
she can help me find a new favorite dessert!

Spell you later,

Raven